THE LADY WHO PUT
SALT IN HER COFFEE
And Other Stories

THE LADY WHO PUT SALT IN HER COFFEE

SALT IN HER COFFEE
And Other Stories

from The Peterkin Papers

BY
LUCRETIA P. HALE

THE GROLIER SOCIETY INC. • NEW YORK

CONTENTS

THE LADY WHO PUT
SALT IN HER COFFEE.

HIS was Mrs. Peterkin. It was a mistake. She had poured out a delicious cup of coffee, and, just as she was helping herself to cream, she found she had put in salt instead of sugar! It tasted bad. What should she do? Of course she couldn't drink the coffee; so she called in the family, for she was sitting at a late breakfast all alone.

The family came in; they all tasted, and looked, and wondered what should be done, and all sat down to think.

At last Agamemnon, who had been to college, said, "Why don't we go over and ask the advice of the chemist?" (For the chemist lived over the way, and was a very wise man.)

Mrs. Peterkin said, "Yes," and Mr. Peterkin said, "Very well," and all the children said they would go too. So the little boys put on their India-rubber boots, and over they went.

Now the chemist was just trying to find out something which should turn everything it touched into gold; and he had a large glass bottle into which he put all kinds of gold and silver, and many other valuable things, and melted them all up over the fire, till he had almost found what

he wanted. He could turn things into almost gold. But just now he had used up all the gold that he had round the house, and gold was high. He had used up his wife's gold thimble and his great-grandfather's gold-bowed spectacles; and he had melted up the gold head of his great-great-grandfather's cane; and, just as the Peterkin family came in, he was down on his knees before his wife, asking her to let him have her wedding ring to melt up with all the rest, because this time he knew he should succeed, and should be able to turn everything into gold; and then she could have a new wedding-ring of diamonds, all set in emeralds and rubies and topazes, and all the furniture could be turned into the finest of gold.

Now his wife was just consenting when the Peterkin family burst in. You can imag-

ine how mad the chemist was! He came near throwing his crucible — that was the name of his melting-pot — at their heads. But he didn't. He listened as calmly as he could to the story of how Mrs. Peterkin had put salt in her coffee.

At first he said he couldn't do anything about it; but when Agamemnon said they would pay in gold if he would only go, he packed up his bottles in a leather case, and went back with them all.

First he looked at the coffee, and then stirred it. Then he put in a little chlorate of potassium, and the family tried it all round; but it tasted no better. Then he stirred in a little bichlorate of magnesia. But Mrs. Peterkin didn't like that. Then he added some tartaric acid and some hyper-sulphate of lime. But no; it was no better. "I have it!" exclaimed the chemist, — "a

little ammonia is just the thing!" No, it wasn't the thing at all.

Then he tried, each in turn, some oxalic, cyanic, acetic, phosphoric, chloric, hyperchloric, sulphuric, boracic, silicic, nitric, formic, nitrous nitric, and carbonic acids. Mrs. Peterkin tasted each, and said the flavor was pleasant, but not precisely that of coffee. So then he tried a little calcium, aluminum, barium, and strontium, a little clear bitumen, and a half of a third of a sixteenth of a grain of arsenic. This gave rather a pretty color; but still Mrs. Peterkin ungratefully said it tasted of anything but coffee. The chemist was not discouraged. He put in a little belladonna and atropine, some granulated hydrogen, some potash, and a very little antimony, finishing off with a little pure carbon. But still Mrs. Peterkin was not satisfied.

The chemist said that all he had done ought to have taken out the salt. The theory remained the same, although the experiment had failed. Perhaps a little starch would have some effect. If not, that was all the time he could give. He should like to be paid, and go. They were all much obliged to him, and willing to give him $1.37½ in gold. Gold was now 2.69¾, so Mr. Peterkin found in the newspaper. This gave Agamemnon a pretty little sum. He sat himself down to do it. But there was the coffee! All sat and thought awhile, till Elizabeth Eliza said, "Why don't we go to the herb-woman?" Elizabeth Eliza was the only daughter. She was named after her two aunts, — Elizabeth, from the sister of her father; Eliza, from her mother's sister. Now, the herb-woman was an old woman who came round to sell herbs, and knew a

great deal. They all shouted with joy at the idea of asking her, and Solomon John and the younger children agreed to go and find her too. The herb-woman lived down at the very end of the street; so the boys put on their India-rubber boots again, and they set off. It was a long walk through the village, but they came at last to the herb-woman's house, at the foot of a high hill. They went through her little garden. Here she had marigolds and hollyhocks, and old maids and tall sunflowers, and all kinds of sweet-smelling herbs, so that the air was full of tansy-tea and elder-blow. Over the porch grew a hop-vine, and a brandy-cherry tree shaded the door, and a luxuriant cranberry-vine flung its delicious fruit across the window. They went into a small parlor, which smelt very spicy. All around hung little bags full of catnip, and pepper-

mint, and all kinds of herbs; and dried stalks hung from the ceiling; and on the shelves were jars of rhubarb, senna, manna, and the like.

But there was no little old woman. She had gone up into the woods to get some more wild herbs, so they all thought they would follow her, — Elizabeth Eliza, Solomon John, and the little boys. They had to climb up over high rocks, and in among huckleberry-bushes and blackberry-vines. But the little boys had their India-rubber boots. At last they discovered the little old woman. They knew her by her hat. It was steeple-crowned, without any vane. They saw her digging with her trowel round a sassafras bush. They told her their story, — how their mother had put salt in her coffee, and how the chemist had made it worse instead of better, and how their mother

couldn't drink it, and wouldn't she come and see what she could do? And she said she would, and took up her little old apron, with pockets all round, all filled with everlasting and pennyroyal, and went back to her house.

There she stopped, and stuffed her huge pockets with some of all the kinds of herbs. She took some tansy and peppermint, and caraway-seed and dill, spearmint and cloves, pennyroyal and sweet marjoram, basil and rosemary, wild thyme and some of the other time, — such as you have in clocks, — sappermint and oppermint, catnip, valerian, and hop; indeed, there isn't a kind of herb you can think of that the little old woman didn't have done up in her little paper bags, that had all been dried in her little Dutch-oven. She packed these all up, and then went back with the children, taking her stick.

Meanwhile Mrs. Peterkin was getting quite impatient for her coffee.

As soon as the little old woman came she had it set over the fire, and began to stir in the different herbs. First she put in a little hop for the bitter. Mrs. Peterkin said it tasted like hop-tea, and not at all like coffee. Then she tried a little flagroot and snakeroot, then some spruce gum, and some caraway and some dill, some rue and rosemary, some sweet marjoram and sour, some oppermint and sappermint, a little spearmint and peppermint, some wild thyme, and some of the other tame time, some tansy and basil, and catnip and valerian, and sassafras, ginger, and pennyroyal. The children tasted after each mixture, but made up dreadful faces. Mrs. Peterkin tasted, and did the same. The more the old woman stirred, and the more she put in, the worse it all seemed to taste.

So the old woman shook her head, and muttered a few words, and said she must go. She believed the coffee was bewitched. She bundled up her packets of herbs, and took her trowel, and her basket, and her stick, and went back to her root of sassafras, that she had left half in the air and half out. And all she would take for pay was five cents in currency.

Then the family were in despair, and all sat and thought a great while. It was growing late in the day, and Mrs. Peterkin hadn't had her cup of coffee. At last Elizabeth Eliza said, "They say that the lady from Philadelphia, who is staying in town, is very wise. Suppose I go and ask her what is best to be done." To this they all agreed, it was a great thought, and off Elizabeth

Eliza went.

She told the lady from Philadelphia the whole story, — how her mother had put salt in the coffee; how the chemist had been called in; how he tried everything but could make it no better; and how they went for the little old herb-woman, and how she had tried in vain, for her mother couldn't drink the coffee. The lady from Philadelphia listened very attentively, and then said, "Why doesn't your mother make a fresh cup of coffee?" Elizabeth Eliza started with surprise. Solomon John shouted with joy; so did Agamemnon, who had just finished his sum; so did the little boys, who had followed on. "Why didn't we think of that?" said Elizabeth Eliza; and they all went back to their mother, and she had her cup of coffee.

ABOUT ELIZABETH
ELIZA'S PIANO

ABOUT ELIZABETH
ELIZA'S PIANO.

LIZABETH ELIZA had a present of a piano, and she was to take lessons from the postmaster's daughter.

They decided to have the piano set across the window in the parlor, and the movers brought it in, and went away.

After they had gone the family all came in to look at the piano; but they found the movers had placed it with its back turned towards the middle of the room, standing close against the window.

How could Elizabeth Eliza open it? How could she reach the keys to play upon it?

Solomon John proposed that they should open the window, which Agamemnon could do with his long arms. Then Elizabeth Eliza should go round upon the piazza, and open the piano. Then she could have her music stool on the piazza, and play upon the piano there.

So they tried this; and they all thought it was a very pretty sight to see Elizabeth Eliza playing on the piano, while she sat on the piazza, with the honeysuckle vines behind her.

It was very pleasant, too, moonlight evenings. Mr. Peterkin liked to take a doze on

his sofa in the room; but the rest of the family liked to sit on the piazza. So did Elizabeth Eliza, only she had to have her back to the moon.

All this did very well through the summer; but, when the fall came, Mr. Peterkin thought the air was too cold from the open window, and the family did not want to sit out on the piazza.

Elizabeth Eliza practiced in the mornings with her coat on; but she was obliged to give up her music in the evenings the family shivered so.

One day, when she was talking with the lady from Philadelphia, she spoke of this trouble.

The lady from Philadelphia looked surprised, and then said, "But why don't you turn the piano round?"

One of the little boys pertly said, "It is

a square piano."

But Elizabeth Eliza went home directly, and, with the help of Agamemnon and Solomon John, turned the piano round.

"Why did we not think of that before?" said Mrs. Peterkin. "What shall we do when the lady from Philadelphia goes home again?"

THE PETERKINS TRY
TO BECOME WISE.

HEY were sitting round the breakfast-table, and wondering what they should do because the lady from Philadelphia had gone away. "If," said Mrs. Peterkin, "we could only be more wise as a family!" How could they manage it? Agamemnon had been to college, and the children all went to school; but still as a family they were not wise. "It comes from books," said one of the family. "People who have a great many books are very wise." Then they counted up that there were very few books in the house, — a few schoolbooks and Mrs. Peterkin's cookbook were all.

"That's the thing!" said Agamemnon. "We want a library."

"We want a library!" said Solomon John. And all of them exclaimed, "We want a library!"

"Let us think how we shall get one," said Mrs. Peterkin. "I have observed that other people think a great deal of thinking."

So they all sat and thought a great while.

Then said Agamemnon, "I will make a library. There are some boards in the woodshed, and I have a hammer and some nails, and perhaps we can borrow

some hinges, and there we have our library!"

They were all very much pleased at the idea.

"That's the bookcase part," said Elizabeth Eliza; "but where are the books?"

So they sat and thought a little while, when Solomon John exclaimed, "I will make a book!"

They all looked at him in wonder.

"Yes," said Solomon John, "books will make us wise; but first I must make a book."

So they went into the parlor, and sat down to make a book. But there was no ink. What should he do for ink? Elizabeth Eliza said she had heard that nutgalls and vinegar made very good ink. So they decided to make some. The little boys said they could find some nutgalls up in the

woods. So they all agreed to set out and pick some. Mrs. Peterkin put on her cape-bonnet, and the little boys got into their India-rubber boots, and off they went.

The nutgalls were hard to find. There was almost everything else in the woods,— chestnuts and walnuts, and small hazel-nuts, and a great many squirrels; and they had to walk a great way before they found any nutgalls. At last they came home with a large basket and two nutgalls in it. Then came the question of the vinegar. Mrs. Peterkin had used her very last on some beets they had the day before. "Suppose we go and ask the minister's wife," said Elizabeth Eliza. So they all went to the minister's wife. She said if they wanted some good vinegar they had better set a barrel of cider down in the cellar, and in a year or two it would make very nice vine-

gar. But they said they wanted it that very afternoon. When the minister's wife heard this she said she should be very glad to let them have some vinegar, and gave them a cupful to carry home.

So they stirred in the nutgalls, and by the time evening came they had very good ink.

Then Solomon John wanted a pen. Agamemnon had a steel one, but Solomon John said, "Poets always used quills." Elizabeth Eliza suggested that they should go out to the poultry-yard and get a quill. But it was already dark. They had, however, two lanterns, and the little boys borrowed the neighbors'. They set out in procession for the poultry yard. When they got there the fowls were all at roost, so they could look at them quietly. But there were no geese! There were Shanghais, and

Cochin-Chinas, and Guinea hens, and Barbary hens, and speckled hens, and Poland roosters, and bantams, and ducks, and turkeys, but not one goose! "No geese but ourselves," said Mrs. Peterkin, wittily, as they returned to the house. The sight of this procession roused up the village. "A torchlight procession!" cried all the boys of the town; and they gathered round the house, shouting for the flag; and Mr. Peterkin had to invite them in, and give them cider and gingerbread, before he could explain to them that it was only his family visiting his hens.

After the crowd had dispersed Solomon John sat down to think of his writing again. Agamemnon agreed to go over to the bookstore to get a quill. They all went over with him. The bookseller was just shutting up his shop. However, he agreed to go in

and get a quill, which he did, and they hurried home.

So Solomon John sat down again, but there was no paper. And now the bookstore was shut up. Mr. Peterkin suggested that the mail was about in, and perhaps he should have a letter, and then they could use the envelope to write upon. So they all went to the post office, and the little boys had their India-rubber boots on, and they all shouted when they found Mr. Peterkin had a letter. The postmaster inquired what they were shouting about; and when they told him he said he would give Solomon John a whole sheet of paper for his book. And they all went back rejoicing.

So Solomon John sat down, and the family all sat round the table looking at him. He had his pen, his ink, and his paper.

He dipped his pen into the ink and held it over the paper, and thought a minute, and then said, "But I haven't got anything to say."

MRS. PETERKIN WISHES
TO GO TO DRIVE.

MRS. PETERKIN WISHES
TO GO TO DRIVE.

NE morning Mrs. Peter-
kin was feeling very
tired, as she had been
having a great many
things to think of,
and she said to Mr.
Peterkin, "I believe I
shall take a ride this morning!"

And the little boys cried out, "Oh, may
we go too?"

Mrs. Peterkin said that Elizabeth Eliza

and the little boys might go.

So Mr. Peterkin had the horse hitched to the carriage, and he and Agamemnon went off to their business, and Solomon John to school; and Mrs. Peterkin began to get ready for her ride.

She had some currants she wanted to carry to old Mrs. Twomly, and some gooseberries for somebody else, and Elizabeth Eliza wanted to pick some flowers to take to the minister's wife; so it took them a long time to prepare.

The little boys went out to pick the currants and the gooseberries, and Elizabeth Eliza went out for her flowers, and Mrs. Peterkin put on her cape-bonnet, and in time they were all ready. The little boys were in their India-rubber boots, and they got into the carriage.

Elizabeth Eliza was to drive; so she sat

on the front seat, and took up the reins, and the horse started off merrily, and then suddenly stopped, and would not go any farther.

Elizabeth Eliza shook the reins, and pulled them, and then she clucked to the horse; and Mrs. Peterkin clucked; and the little boys whistled and shouted; but still the horse would not go.

"We shall have to whip him," said Elizabeth Eliza.

Now Mrs. Peterkin never liked to use the whip; but, as the horse would not go, she said she would get out and turn his head the other way, while Elizabeth Eliza whipped the horse, and when he began to go she would hurry and get in.

So they tried this, but the horse would not stir.

"Perhaps we have too heavy a load,"

said Mrs. Peterkin, as she got in.

So they took out the currants and the gooseberries and the flowers, but still the horse would not go.

One of the neighbors, from the opposite house, looking out just then, called out to them to try the whip. There was a high wind, and they could not hear exactly what she said.

"I have tried the whip," said Elizabeth Eliza.

"She says 'whips,' such as you eat," said one of the little boys.

"We might make those," said Mrs. Peterkin, thoughtfully.

"We have got plenty of cream," said Elizabeth Eliza.

"Yes, let us have some whips," cried the little boys, getting out.

And the opposite neighbor cried out

something about whips; and the wind was very high.

So they went into the kitchen, and whipped up the cream, and made some very delicious whips; and the little boys tasted all round, and they all thought they were very nice.

They carried some out to the horse, who swallowed it down very quickly.

"That is just what he wanted," said Mrs. Peterkin; "now he will certainly go!"

So they all got into the carriage again, and put in the currants, and the gooseberries, and the flowers; and Elizabeth Eliza shook the reins, and they all clucked; but still the horse would not go!

"We must either give up our ride," said Mrs. Peterkin, mournfully, "or else send over to the lady from Philadelphia, and see what she will say."

The little boys jumped out as quickly as they could; they were eager to go and ask the lady from Philadelphia. Elizabeth Eliza went with them, while her mother took the reins.

They found that the lady from Philadelphia was very ill that day, and was in her bed. But when she was told what the trouble was she very kindly said they might draw up the curtain from the window at the foot of the bed, and open the blinds, and she would see. Then she asked for her operaglass, and looked through it, across the way, up the street, to Mrs. Peterkin's door.

After she had looked through the glass she laid it down, leaned her head back against the pillow, for she was very tired, and then said, "Why don't you unchain the horse from the hitching post?"

Elizabeth Eliza and the little boys looked at one another, and then hurried back to the house and told their mother. The horse was untied, and they all went to ride.

Other Books You Will Enjoy